WHEN
TIME
WAS
BORN

BY
JAMES T. FARRELL
DRAWINGS
BY
STEPHEN DWOSKIN

THE SMITH

BY ARRANGEMENT WITH HORIZON PRESS

for Cleo Paturis

INTRODUCTION

1

When Time Was Born was written in about twenty consecutive hours in 1959. It was written in one draft, but it has since been edited three or four times, by myself. I have made only small revisions, in all of my editing. Anyone interested can compare the present and final version with the work as it was first published, under the title of "Prose Poem," in *The American Book Collector*, summer/fall issue, 1961.

There I stated that "Prose Poem" was part of volume 2 of *A Universe of Time*, the long series of novels on which I have been working since October 21st, 1958. However, I changed my plan and published that novel, *What Time Collects*, without this work included.

It seemed to me best to do this, because I had no hope of gaining much understanding, and I feared that this prose poem might be lost in the novel. My decision seems to have been a sound one.

What Time Collects is not about Chicago, nor about the Irish and Irish-Americans. Yet, some managed to say that it is. The writing is far different from that in *Studs Lonigan*. Yet many managed to say that it isn't. The patterns of time in *What Time Collects* and in *Studs Lonigan* are far different, but some managed to say otherwise.

There were these and related reasons to persuade me. Another reason then came into play.

The publisher for my novel did not seem to care.

I could just as well keep my gift. I was certain that I would be the gainer in the long run.

And furthermore, I did not see why I should not let my critics trip themselves. They were still thinking about Studs Lonigan, and many were saying that I would write nothing else. My future failure was being predicted, dogmatically, arbitrarily.

I was certain that *When Time Was Born* would be published sooner or later.

With a single stroke, I would sweep around their careless ends, and score the touchdown that would be my victory.

7

Now, it is published. It puts the seal upon positions which I have held for a number of these last years. I waited for someone who would see the value of this prose poem and publish it for itself. I found such a person in *The Smith*.

After *The Smith* had agreed to publish this prose poem, I gave it the title, *When Time Was Born*.

When Time Was Born gained me a new friendship and a collaborator in publishing works that might otherwise languish in gray boxes and on dusty shelves.

2

How did I happen to write *When Time Was Born*? "Happen" is the correct word to employ here. There is a clear sense in which I can say that *When Time Was Born* happened to be written.

The idea for this prose poem came as I was writing. I had begun my massive series, *A Universe of Time*, on October 21st, 1958, in the early a.m., about 1 a.m. to 2 a.m. I started to write either a novel or a novelette. What I wrote impressed me. As a writer, I have never over-estimated myself. Over-estimation is worse than under-estimation. I have always been cautious about the estimation of myself as a writer. Writing is too serious to me that I should concern myself with self-flattery, especially adjectives in the superlative degree. Self-flattery as a habit is folly; it can even be a superlative degree of folly.

But after I had begun on October 21st, I lifted my estimation of my capabilities. I knew that I was ready for work which I had held in abeyance. As far back as 1932 and 1933, I declared that I was one day going to do writing for which I was not then ready. My writing about certain locales in Chicago, about characters from this locale, about environments which I had assimilated to a degree of relative saturation—this was a beginning. That is how I saw my writing. I was, from the start, which I date to early in 1927, preparing myself for future work. This is one reason, but not the only one, for my extensive reading. I learned, in those days, that many people do not give advice to a writer, they monger it. They monger advice that, if taken, can be fatal to growth, the integrity of a writer's work.

My first book, *Young Lonigan*, was published in 1932. I noted a number of reviews containing errors of fact. The environment in which young Studs Lonigan lives was falsely characterized. Thus, it was called a slum. There was one review in *The New York Times Book Review* which gave the public advice that I had written all there was to say about my subject and that I should write something else. I had more than four other books written. One of these four was, substantially, and a little more than substantially, *The Young Manhood of Studs Lonigan*.

In 1933, my second novel, *Gas House McGinty,* was published. In the same newspaper I read that it was repetitive of *Young Lonigan.* I knew better.

Furthermore, reviewers from the start have explained my my purpose. I did not know them, nor they, me. I was self-conscious, and I knew what I wanted to do. It did not correspond to what strangers stated as my purpose. I had purposes, not *a* purpose.

Not only would I have confused myself into near idiocy if I had taken this stuff seriously, I would also, probably, have lost my sanity.

3

At the time that I wrote this prose poem, I had no contract for the books of my new series. In this sense, I did not have a publisher. I was not writing one novel in a series, to be followed by the next in that series, as had been my practice in the past. I was writing a continuous narrative, exposition, and succession of stories, and of stories within stories. I had abandoned the pattern of chronological time sequences, with a presentation of characters and events from the standpoint of immediate experience, and with the characters revealing themselves *sans* auctinal comment. This is the means I employed in writing my other novels.

The fact that I should change my methods should not be unusual, startling, surprising. Such an effect of surprise is likely among those who have fictionalized me into a commonplace. But those, of this kidney, long ago told me what they were. I ask myself—is there not some pathos mixed in with the comic aspects of those who become dogmatic and absolutistic about clichés?

It is safer to rape the wives of many than it is to rape their clichés. I have raped neither, but I arouse people, not by intention, however. I arouse people because I'll not practice the policy of trying to be as others think I am or as they want me to be.

Why is this?

This is a question I leave for others to explain. I shall, nevertheless, give one suggestion about those who have apprehensions in their clichés. They save themselves from thinking and feeling by accepting clichés which need not be accepted. Clichés leave hollowness, a vacuum in the minds of those who rely on them. The hollowness, the vacuum, explodes if clichés are seriously menaced. This is not a law that always works. It is a generalization about fair frequency. And I suggest, therefore, that the surprised turn their eyes upon the sources of their surprise.

4

An artist tries to fulfill his potentialities.

The critics, reviewers and many others have been obstacles.

Many who praised and hailed my work, most especially *Studs Lonigan,* have been obstacles as great as those who attacked me.

They type cast me.

To create misunderstanding is an intellectual imposition and presumption that adds up to staggering burdens upon others. Such criticism hurts literature, especially in a time of rampant commercialism which continues at a pace which the rapacious constantly accelerate. But the practice is so common that many fall lightly into it. The seriousness, the burdensomeness, the waste of time and money of those who accept misunderstanding as truth—this needs to be pointed out clearly.

The critics are said to be having their day now. In a sense, this is true, but this sense is not that the pendulum has swung and we live in an age of critics and of criticism. Such generalizations are logically poor and off-balance. The pendulum is a cliché—a cheapened verbalism.

This is an age of expanded and intensified competition among creative writers, and for them. This being so, it does not follow that the conditions of competition should determine what the creative writer does. Such conditions should not determine and encompass what he writes and how he writes, whatever he deals with.

I deem this point to be important.

5

The conditions of competition are evident enough. There is the factor of time. Television is an outstanding instance, an alternative means to get that which one gets from reading.

The most serious form of competition between TV and literature involves the form and content of writing.

This competition is an imposed one as far as many writers are concerned. If not many, then some.

Many book and magazine publishers and editors have encouraged writers to write only that which has sales potential for other media.

This is a very sore point with me. I have some regard for my profession. It is an honorable one. I do not underestimate my writing. I do not take with good grace the pressures of publisher and others to have me subordinate my work to the standards, demands, and profits of other media, television and motion pictures in particular. Year after year, I have pursued my profession, and plenty of people can profit enough from my writing. The efforts to inveigle or to pressure me into accepting the criteria, restrictions and equivocations of the other media are unworthy, mean, shameful, petty and parasitic. More, they are exploitive.

If those who do this do not have enough money, let them make call girls out of their wives, mistresses, sweethearts, daughters, nieces and granddaughters. They shall not make a call writer out of me.

I propose to outwrite these media as well as the publishing industry.

The circumstances of competition here are unequal. That I like. Money does not think, and the money men of cultural entrepreneurship (the word is an economic misnomer today) do not imagine.

They can fight me as they wish. They can blacklist me as they wish. They can reject me as they wish.

I guarantee to survive, and, I guarantee that my bones, dissolving into chalky dust, will fight them from the grave.

When Time Was Born is an act of faith.

There shall be more.

James T. Farrell
December 10, 1965

WHEN TIME WAS BORN

Time moved slowly backwards through more than one thousand nine hundred and twenty years of A.D., and five thousand years of A.D. and B.C., through all of the years and years of the Jewish calender, through all of the years of recorded history, through all of the years pre-history, through thousands of years and millenia before millenia, before Hector was a pup, through the Neolithic and Paleolothic ages, back through and before the Darwin man, the Dover man, Pithecanthropus Erectus, and all of the fathers of the fathers of the fathers of the fathers of all of the cave man, and back, back through the millenia of jungles when the apes were beginning to turn themselves into the noblest of all that is born, and lives and breathes and dies upon this whirling earth, and back before the apes and monkeys, the mammals, the dinosaurs, back to the unrecorded days in the timeless time before time was known, back to the day, or the moment, or the non-moment of the non-day of the era of the no-time, back to whenever it was, and wherever it was, and however it was, with the aid of nature, God, and all of the gods that be, as well as blind determinism, heredity and environment, the moon, the shining stars, the blue of the sky, the gold and yellow of the sun, the glories and grandeur of all that is beautiful on land, and on the sea, and in the air, back, back, back and back to the chance moment or non-moment of a chance encounter that became like the living myth, the universal allegory, the profoundly profound ambiguity, the non-ambiguity, the first great moment of beauty in that first second of time, the first soundless tick, the first silent beat, that first, that very, very, and very veriest of infinitesimal fraction of fractions of fractions of the first sound of time when the first tadpole met the first fish in the loveless and universal Proterozoic gloom when all, all was mindless, insensate, back truly to the first moment when the tadpole saw the fish the fish, and the fish first saw the tadpole up the tadpole, and in a period of sight, recognition awakened desire, awakened feeling, a period which might have been long and might have been short because neither poets nor poetry had yet been born, created, in that period, short or long, that time when the stars shone for nothing but themselves, the moon glowed silver for nothing but itself, and the sun shone and burned for nothing but itself, and the sky was blue for nothing but itself, and the sea roared and pulsed, stormed and ebbed into a calm like the calm of the nothingness that the infinite pre-Einsteinian, pre-Newtonian, pre-Gallilean, pre-Copernican, pre-Euclidean, pre-Mosaic, pre-Andrew Jackson Davis, pre-Adam-and-Eve, pre-Genesis, pre-Jehovahan universe—back when all and everything in all of the spaces and beyond the infinity of the regions of stardust, when Venus didn't know herself from Jupiter, Saturn, and the small round planet Earth, back to that union of the tadpole and the fish when the first awakening tadpole made love, romantic and unromantic, to the first awakening fish, and creativity was born, and the first dim and feeble glow of imagination, the first almost unfelt quiver of feeling, the first chill sensation of contact, the first, first, first of these ever-recurrent joys and sorrows which led God to create Eve, and which made Eve and her famous daughters, including Rebecca and Samson's Delilah, the daughters of

Ashkelon, and all the wives of David, and Venus and Helen and Aphrodite, and Isis, and Cleopatra, and even Caesar's wife, and Eleanor of Acquitaine, and Salome, and the wives and women whose memory is briefly chopped and carved in Sumarian stone, and all of the remembered girls and women of all recorded history, even including Socrates' Xantippe, and all of the unrecorded and unremembered girls and women in all of that long and forever lost, forever gone, and forever disappeared universe of time and on into the mists when time was infinitesimally more young than the newborn infant, and the first feeling and the first second of time were born when the tadpole loved the fish and the fish loved the tadpole, and the ocean was blue and inky and its blue was unnamed, and green was unnamed green upon the land, and the tides of the ocean and the restless waves rolled on and on with unheard roars and broke upon the rocks and sands at the edge of land, and the light of dawn was a faint penetration through the darkness that hung over the ocean and over the land, and the tadpole and the fish met and made love, romantic and unromantic, and from that moment when time was young and new, and time was also young with love and love was young with time, and young in time—back through the years, when love grew and became always young and forever old, and worlds and beings and feelings and love and time were forever being born and always dying, and on back through those mists of the unrecorded lost years of the beginning, until that fated and dramatic moment in the Garden of Eden when Adam stood in the naked splendor of all his force and all his strength, an isolated man, innocent in his loneliness, more virginal in the feelings and needs of his manhood than the tadpole and the fish, and out of his strong, young, naked body the Lord God from on high performed the most fateful, the most dramatic, the most spectacular operation in all the history of surgery, and in this operation, God jerked out of Adam, without benefit of knife or anesthesia, a rib, and Eve became the most luscious, the sweetest, the juiciest, the most tender and most tough, the most wonderful flesh that ever has grown or ever will grow and multiply in cells from any rib from among all the ribs there ever were or will be, or from any other bones from among all of the fabulous and uncounted bones that ever supported living flesh and then slowly eroded into white chalky dust and were blown and scattered like bits of ashes in caves and subterranean holes in the earth, and over the plains and mountains, over the valleys, and over the pulsing oceans and the noisy waters, simultaneously monotonous and un-monotonous in all this time of timelessness, of time, of disappearing and emerging time, and bones that were dropped into the earth and that were buried as the monotonous unmonotonous waters made a moan like the ever recurrent, timelessly unsilenced man of eternity, and they have soughed and roared and filled the damp air over the waters and by the water's edge with echoing melancholy of the world and the same waters have filled the same damp spaces of air with the echoing stridences and rhythms which make a music of the strength and force, and the power and careless vigor and the wild, wet exuberance which has been forever and always bursting out of the hidden womb where hides the enemy of all of the worlds of all the time and all of the timelessness, in that always before the beginning, and from the beginning through all the rotations and rhythms which are the meters, the lines of all that natural poetry which we know and feel and taste and hear and touch and hold in our minds as the undying wonder of the world, and the waters of the world have stormed and stormed again in their bursting and violent revelations of that wonder of the world, and while the waters have shattered and reshattered and reshattered the calm man dreams into the blue electric air, all of these unadded and untotaled bones have with fatal tragic slowness turned grain by grain into dust, bleached chalk dust, gray with dusty, dirty gray dust, fine black dust, and dust, indiscriminate dust, the dust of bones more numerous than all of the stars, dust disintegrating back into the hidden womb of all the energy which is the semen of wonder, deathless wonder, the wonder which hangs like a veil fine spun into invisibility, which is spread before the only mystery and the many mysteries of the only mystery, the mystery of life. And that mystery was lost in that which made Adam's rib the one creative bone from among all and all and all the bones that have ever slowly fallen into dust, and all the bones that yet will fall to dust. And the creative mystery in Adam's rib grew into all the wonder that was the flesh of Eve, flesh more juicy than the apple whose red and whose juice have been the stage props of the permanent tragedy of joy and deceptive joy and the illusion of joy and the bitterness that comes when these joys break apart and lay like dust and ashes strewn across our memories. The juicy sweetness of Eve's apple, its succulence, was no less sweet for all its consequence, and sweeter than Eve's apple was Eve's flesh. And Eve's flesh was no less sweet, and soft with wonder and wondrously soft, the living, the sweetest in all the Garden of Eden.

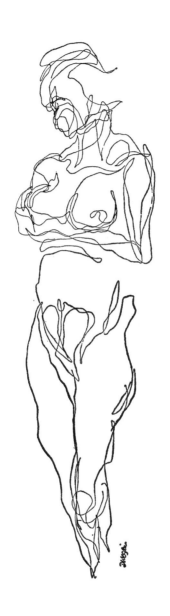

The tadpole and the fish by the water's edge where the thinnest light of dawn slowly warmed a path through the cold dark air and first rays of heat gave the fire of life to the dream that grew in a mystery as deep as the ocean and protected by a wonder as impenetrable as the wonder in every drop of the storming ocean. And that warmed mystery grew into the flames which for a few moments when even disappearing time was a deceit more cruel than the lying tongue of a snake which hid in the greenest grass which ever grew in the mind of any man, the grass of the changeless green of Paradise. And all the poison of the sweetly lying serpent, and all the lies which slid off her tongue like snakes sliding through slime were sweet like the sweetest apple in all the dreams of men and women, and like the green of the greenest grass, and like the tenderness of the flesh on Eve's round and beautiful unsucked breasts. Perhaps not the first tadpole and the first fish, nor the second nor the third, but one tadpole and one fish made love, romantic and unromantic, when all of the world was paradise, and they were composed and lying under sun almost as still as light, thin glass, now green, now blue, lying on the surface of the waters like a microscopic picture of a rare and tiny turquoise stone which has been magnified to the size of the sky and which suddenly but slowly changes and is newly and different with each new second, and which can glow and shine and never be the same for two instants and which is many turquoise splendors just as each star is a surface of many splendors in the sky. And on the shore in a world where there is only beneficent harmony, and all of the sounds of the universe are muted, and if silence could have had an echo, then the water lapping the dark brown and wet sand of the shore line was like the sound of a caress and sound as the echo of a silent kiss of grateful tenderness exchanged by two lovers in the first receding aftermath of the first discovery of the after-peace of love when love is new and their feelings have awakened like sleeping flowers in a garden opening to a sun which is like the first sun that ever beamed—lapping waters, like lapping, lapping while far up and curving out of the nothingness that is beyond the sky, and below the sky, and behind the horizon where the earth, land, and the turquoise waters end like a straight line ruling off the edge between what is land and what is an empty well of space and air. The sky looks as though it had been washed and ironed, celestially laundered until it has become the cleanest, clearest, purest and most spotless sky that ever did or ever will or ever can need or ever should lay upside down above an earth, the sky that was as quiet and unruffled or as a deserted little park untroubled by man or wind on the June day of Harmonious Promise. And the sailing clouds were as white as milk but not the color of milk, but of a purity of white in which there is no other shade nor shadow nor adumbration nor faint trace of any other color, but only the white, the white of clouds sailing like ships across the calmest waters but was shaped like nothing that ever was before or ever will be again, shaped as they had been by vapors winding together and being shredded apart by winds which pushed invisibly from nowhere, crossing atmospheres with a seeming aimlessness greater than the seeming aimlessness of birds seen briefly and fluttering crazily and nervously wriggling towards the destination of nowhere.

The waters lap and the winds shake the trees, and the sky is silent, and the clouds sail, as noiseless as ghosts, and the birds have not yet been born to sing and the animals of the land have as yet been unborn to howl and roar and slaw and kill, and God and all the gods that be have drowsed away in sleep, and invisible in nowhere, the winds sift through the beards of God and all the gods, and at the edge of lapping, lapping waters, the tadpole and the fish, having made love, are drowsy with warmth inside themselves. They are alone together in the world, warm from making love, peaceful from making love, and new feelings awaken one by one, like notes of music in a minor key because they have made love and have gained a feeling of peace inside themselves and within one another, and the wind blows over them and against them but it soothes and does not sting. Just as love has soothed them and they have become so quiet in themselves that the slow and simple, the old and new, thoughts and feelings sail within them as silently as the clouds are sailing in the sky, and just as the clouds have come together as drifting vapors, so have the feelings of the tadpole and the fish come together, like vapors becoming clouds, propelled by the first stirrings of the winds of infant consciousness within them.

From love to love, romantic and unromantic, from tadpole and fish to tadpole and fish, the inner wind of consciousness grew stronger, slowly, very slowly, but it grew little by little. And in the changing, never fully still universe the turn to blackness, which was later called "the night," was never the same blackness, the same darkness, the same absence of light and color, the same monstrous mass of thick shapelessness which simulated shape, and then the faintest gray reflections of what was not black and colorless, and the lazy play of blue and white and almost white, and the nuances of the colors of light, which was later called the dawn.

And the red red of the sky, redder than Eve's apple, was born out of the disappearing darkness. And then what was later called the dawn came up like silent thunder out of a nameless somewhere across the spaceless sky from a seashore without a name when the wonders of the world were wonders of a world where time had but begun and was not yet even young. The dawn came up like silent thunder, but the thunders of the sky were not, and the streaks of lightning were not, and the clouds were too empty for rain, and love came new for that tadpole and that fish that were not the first or the second tadpoles and fishes to pair together and to make love. But the tadpole and fish of the gray dawn when time was infant were the first tadpole and the first fish to discover, in the languorous and sweetly dreaming aftermath of love, the peace of slow, caressing change when the warm and warming and more warmly growing winds of consciousness go so slow that time is going slow and slowly into sleep. And when time is slow in love's aftermath, and all the moving vapors and clouds, and all the change within the lovers fatigued into some awakeness, some dreaming in awakeness, some dreaming with awakeness and sleeping, and some dreaming in sleeping, and some sleeping, and then one time becomes more than one time, and other times come back in the dreams of half-sleeping, and sleeping and half-being-awake in other times and other times, and in half awakening, there is another time and still other times, carrying different thoughts, feelings, images, and a dream grows from these images torn from the many times and different times, and becomes the dream of no time, and that is paradise, the garden where all is peace, the time when love is sweet, and when to die is not to die but to live on the sweetness of the aftermath, and Eden is the garden of love, fulfilled when the storms of passing time have rolled into the smooth sandy beaches of fulfillment, and love seems sweeter than the sweetest and the reddest red apple that ever deceived man and woman.

And thus, there was the tadpole and the fish in whom love found its loveliest habitat, a Garden of Eden growing in the mind and located out there, across Nowhere and many Somewheres, a garden where green is the greenest green, and red the reddest red, and even the snake in the grass with the polished tongue that utters poisonous fraud is a friend, and all of the world is this garden, and the winds kiss and the waters caress, and the thunders are silent, and the sky is still and the sky is the clearest sky that ever cast light upon the world. And thus it was for a tadpole and a fish after love had begun between the first tadpole and the first fish in the ocean's slime and the dawn came with thunders cracking the air until the atmosphere and all of the dark infinities of space were shattered and the world was a wonder of screeching, screaming, violent, monotonous change that seemed to split the seconds of time like wrecked and broken atoms, and that first tadpole and that first fish found love and only a feeble glow of warmth in chill and darkness. And thus they were alone together, with love giving birth to their first seconds of time, awakening with their first flickerings of feeling for the first time telling them that they existed. And they knew, after their chance encounter and their love, that they were different. They lived in the before and in the after, in nothing and the beginning, and the beginning was the first second of time and love.

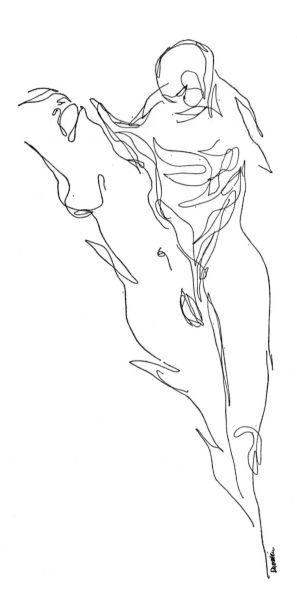

And thus it was, when all of the world was peaceful and the tadpole and the fish, but not the first tadpole and the first fish, were awakened by the first fragment of the dream of love which is paradise, all of the world was paradise, and all of the world was an image of paradise. They were not alone together, but they were alone in the world. The feeling of Paradise was in them, and the image of Paradise was the world and the sky, the wind, the water, the lapping and caressing sounds, the silently moving clouds, and they were no longer a little tadpole and a little fish, but the tadpole and the fish that found the beauty of the world in themselves, and the beauty of their aftermath in the beauty of the world.

And the day of the tadpole and the fish, when Paradise was all of the world and Paradise was how that tadpole and that fish felt, the day when Paradise was all of the changes that are the facts of time, that day disappeared and was no more, and the tadpole disappeared and the fish disappeared and they were no more. And many bones had begun their millenial decomposition and devolution into dust and ashes, ashy dust and dusty ashes.

And out of time, the Garden of Eden was alive with more colors than any rainbow that ever beamed down from the sky. And in song and color and sun, Adam roamed the Garden, a man alone, master and lord of Paradise. There was no time because there was no change in Paradise. Adam in the peace of Paradise was as much alone as the first tadpole in the slime of the pitching ocean until the first tadpole met the first fish.

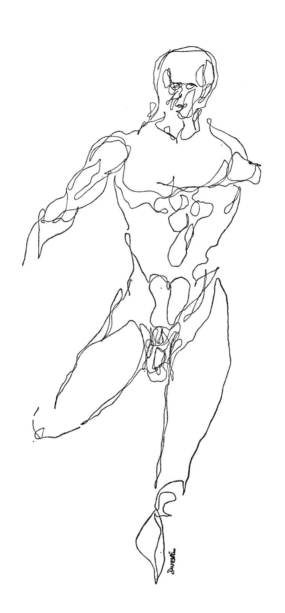

Walking about in the Garden of Eden, Adam was as natural as the sun. He was at one with all the fish and fowl, the birds and beasts: he was at one with all the world. He knew the names of all the animals and he could speak to them, and they could speak to him. He could ask the fish how the water was and they could tell him that the water was always warm, but never too warm. He walked about the Garden of Eden, through all the paths, in the shadowy woods, by the edge of a pool of water that was clean and pure.

It was a small blue pool or a large blue lake, fresh and clear and with a surface polished and ruffled only when a fish now and then would leap out of the water, make a small splash and break the blue polish with jagged white foam. The birds of paradise were singing, not in chorus, but with many separate voices, mingling their notes, their warblings and chirpings, their songs and sounds clashing in the air, and in the woods beyond the like where bushy trees and tall, straight ones stood in a contrast of majesty and coloring, a wonder of sun and shade, of glare and shadow for the many friends of Adam, the species that would multiply according to the High Command of Jehovah, the old but ageless God with a beard of cleanest white and with eyes that saw all and saw too much. From the forest in Paradise, more singing came breaking through the trees, floating through the soft air, and more of warbling, more chirping, more of the song and sound of the birds who, like the fishes, were the friends of Adam. And from far in the forest came a growing, growling, mounting roar, deep and tense, angry and powerful, rolling in big, unseen, perturbing waves through the leaves, towards the like, crossing the motionless air above the motionless water, and the roar of the lion carried through the trees on the opposite shore, fading, losing volume, diminishing, a dimming echo of the majestic power of the monarch of the forest. And while the birds and animals continued their cacophony, the majestic roar of the monarch of the forest was swallowed up somewhere in nowhere, out beyond the Garden where a pitiless sun was bleaching and burning more whiteness on the hot and lifeless white bones uncounted and forgotten as all of the earth and all of the world and all of the universe was becoming a new universe, and the work of change and changing continued, marking time by the shadows of the sun which carelessly played on the careening planet, Earth. And time was old and time was in all the bright and all of the blue reaches where stillness is but unseen motion, and in an infinity of space, where there is no permanence for fish nor fowl, animal nor man, and where death is not death but one more change. And time, and time, and time was measured off in drops of water falling on rocks, dripping, wearing away, disappearing infinitesimal pieces of rock, pieces that would be as invisible to the eye of Adam, the only man in the universe, as he would be invisible from the hot, feelingless sun.

The universe of the day when the first tadpole and the first fish met in their brief new encounter was no more and a new universe was becoming another new universe, and in the Garden of Eden, Adam, the first man, walked, upright, brown and handsome, with a black beard and long black hair. And his manliness and his manhood were less to him, the first man, than the organs of all the men who were to follow Adam and make their contributions to the process of increasing and multiplying. Adam walked, innocent, the first and most unself-conscious of all the men that ever would be. And he walked with strong and vigorous step, still the first man and he didn't know what to do with his full and healthy young manhood.

The Garden of Eden was not in time and what is not in time is not changing and what is not changing is not, and what is not is not existing, and what is not existing is but a dream, a fantasy—and that was Adam.

Adam, our first ancestor, our common father, was flesh and blood, and every organ of him was good, his heart was good, his veins were good, his liver was good, his digestion was good, his eyes were good and clear and dark, his teeth were good and white and sharp and even, his muscles rippled good under his skin, his skin was good and brown and smooth, the smoothest skin in Paradise, and he heard the little noises and the big cacophony, and he heard the words of the Lord God Jehovah, and he heard the animals, and Adam was a particular kind of composition of chemical elements which, in Paradise, would have sold for nothing because there was neither mankind nor money, nor buyer nor seller, nor profit nor loss.

Adam was young and indestructible, and it is certain that he must have been more perfectly formed than any of the young men down through all the ages who were golden lads for a time and have now gone nowhere into dust, along with chimney sweepers, poor Yorrick, and the first tadpole and the first fish and the other hordes who have gone down the dusty death. There would never again be as perfectly formed, created, constructed, proportioned and rounded a youth as the first of all the golden lads who, like chimney sweepers, have gone to dust. For Adam, unlike the millions of youths who followed him over the ages, was not born of woman but was fashioned full by the sure Hand of God. Adam with the long hair, the strong and sturdy and vigorous body, Adam, the one mortal being whom God Himself created, could walk and could talk, after a fashion, to the fish under the water, the fowl in the air, the birds in the trees, and the beasts in the forest. But how much could he say to them? Unlike the tadpole, he couldn't cuddle up because in the Proterozoic Era when the first Adam was a tadpole and his Eve was a fish, they were at the very beginning of the beginning, and they began at the beginning. But on the Seventh Day, Man was created, and Man was Adam. And in all of the six days when the aged but ageless Lord God, Jehovah, labored in the creation of his masterpiece, Adam was not there nor anywhere. Unlike all their descendants, only Adam and his Eve did not come the usual way. Adam was the appearance of God's Platonism, a man molded in the image and likeness of the idea. Adam had not become Adam as a seed going into the womb, a wriggling little tadpole of a seed entering the ovum and enriching the egg. But what is love? Adam did not know.

And God created Adam as His final achievement. Adam came after night and day, the sky, the firmament, the earth, the planets, the bananas and the figs and the olives and the flowers and the birds and the bees and the fowl and geese and all that flies in the air and all of the animals in the forest and everything in all of the created world. Adam was the last and the last was first. The Garden of Eden was his to enjoy as enjoy he might or could. Paradise was Adam's but it was not quite Adam's. For God had made Adam to supervise as well as enjoy and Adam, a man alone in the Garden of Eden, was something of a zoo keeper and the overseer of a garden. He did not have much to do in supervising the zoo because the beasts of the field didn't seem to cause any trouble in Paradise and food was available without the keeper providing it. The flowers needed no watering nor tending and Adam needed merely to look at them as Adam wished and to smell their perfume if Adam also wished. Adam of course had capacities as we know because when his days in Paradise abruptly ended and the angels drove him into the world of time, he fumed and did plenty of sweating and he became an almost record breaking begetter, perhaps a better begetter than any of the rest of the Adams who have come after him. But Adam, the unbegetter, did not as then know how much begetting there was unused in his loins and he did not seem to know much else. Wandering about in the fabulous garden amidst the wonders and beauties of all the natural world, saying something but not much to a whale or a perch, perhaps asking the first jackass if jackassing was jackassing, there Adam was, newly made, a living and breathing statue in the beauteous and luxuriant Garden of Eden and still as naked as on the Seventh Day when God, Jehovah, picked up that handful of dust and fashioned this healthy and well-made walking and talking statue, but in the first moments of his life, there was none of the Old Adam in Adam. He was a man but immortal because he had not eaten the fruit of the Tree of Knowledge and of life, and without past, his future was his present. He could go on talking to the fish.

But the Lord God said to the Lord God, that is to himself, that it was not good for Adam to be alone. Thus it happened that Adam was put into a long sleep, and when he woke up, he did not miss the rib which the Lord God had painlessly removed from his chest, and there was Eve, and as new and as naked as Adam. But Eve was not then Eve, but only Woman. She was Woman because Adam was Man and Woman was of Man, that is of Adam, his flesh and his bones, because Woman was what God could do with one of the ribs of Man. And God had done this with a rib instead of dust because God had made Woman for Man. Thus it was and it was so, in the Garden of Eden, called Paradise.

But the Lord God had not told Eve what she could do and what she dare not do as he had told Adam. The Lord God made Woman for Man, the Woman who would then soon be known as Eve for Adam and it was for Adam to tell her.

And Adam was naked and Woman was naked and they were not ashamed. But there was nothing to be ashamed of. For Woman knew less than Man, and Man, Adam, had no means of knowing more than what he had been told. For Jehovah had made Adam for Himself, and Woman for Man.

It appears that having gotten a Woman, a mate, a wife at the painless cost of one rib, removed in a deep sleep, while the fish were fish, and the bees were bees, and the birds were birds, and the beasts of the fields were beasts of the fields, Man, Adam, knew he should leave his father, and leave his mother and cleave to his own flesh, Woman, but Adam had no father but God, and Adam had no mother, and naked and without shame, Man, Adam, and the flesh of his flesh, the bone of his bone, Woman. Adam lived a long and healthy, if a hard and sweating and begetting life, and that long life of Adam was not rendered less long because Man, Adam, the first man had one rib less than all of the sons of Adam were to have when there came to pass what did come to pass.

And it was so that Man, Adam and not Man because he was Adam, got a Woman for a rib and the Woman was his. And Adam and the Woman, that is, the flesh of his lost rib, the bone of his lost rib, the hair of his lost rib, the eyes and all that was Woman, naked and without shame, were man and mate in the Garden of Eden, Paradise.

And the Garden of Eden was a tropical Paradise, where snow was unknown and Adam and that bone of his bone, and flesh of his flesh, that transformed missing rib of his, did not even know what snow and cold and rain and wind and the rawness of the elements were or could be. And there was no thunder other than the thunder which

could be in the voice of the Lord God who made Adam as the prized creation of all of his creations, including the Garden of Eden, and Who had made Woman for Adam.

There was no work to do and Adam thus had no need to earn his bread by the sweat of his brow, and if there were any sweat on Adam's brow, it was merely caused by the heat. But in Paradise, the tropical heat would have been modified and the first Man and the first Woman would not have sweltered and suffered the painful rigors of the heat of the sun. Paradise cannot be Paradise if there be suffering within it. The atmosphere in Paradise could only have been as divine as is imagined to be divine the legendary nectar of the gods. It might have been called ambrosial weather. Paradise was God-created, and the Lord God Jehovah Himself had said unto Himself that all that He had made was good.

And it was so.

It was so that in the beginning when Adam and his Woman were in the Garden God had made and given into the care of Adam, and the two of them were in their home, Man's first home, the atmosphere was what only the Lord God Himself had ordered. And never on Mount Parnassus could the mythological Zeus have ordered it better for the comfort of his afternoons and evenings when he would preside at the table of the gods and goddesses, the company of the Immortals would feast and sport as only the Immortals knew how to make sport. Nor

53

could Venus herself have made the atmosphere more languorous, with the air sweet but just thick enough and heavy enough to seduce into drowsy languor, to numb with caressing fingers of heat but not to torment with heat that is as heavy as lead within a man's head. The very air was sensuous, full of a seductiveness for all of the senses of man. It was an air that intoxicates, an air of champagne that penetrated every pore and affected the mind so that the dreams within were like all of the world men see with their eyes and contact with all of their senses. It was an air which dulled but did not depress the mind so that it was in tune, in harmony, in an accord of dreams and visions with all that was in the Garden. It was an air for the poet, Keats, who was to be born and to live his few brief days millenial afterwards, and it were as though a lingering memory of the air and atmosphere of the Garden of Eden slept on and slept on and on and on while there was Sumer, and Egypt, and Nineveah and Troy and Babylon, and Assyria and Phoenicia and Persia and all of the East and of the Indies and of the New Indies, and the chosen of the Lord Himself led by His Prophet Moses, and all of that glory that was Greece, and Rome, a memory that slept somewhere until the Seven Wonders of the World were cracked and cracking ruins and where Socrates walked was warm grass and black dirt, and where conquering glory that was Rome was but ruined and wrecked arches and broken stones, in a sunken earth, and the sons of Adam and the daughters of Eve had seen the majesty drop into the nothingness that is all of their yesterdays and all of our yesterdays, and that sleeping memory awoke only in the mind of a young, consumptive and doomed poet on an island near to a continent, and he felt that "drowsy numbness" which was in the air when Adam, naked and without shame, first looked at what the Lord God, Himself, could do with the rib of a man.

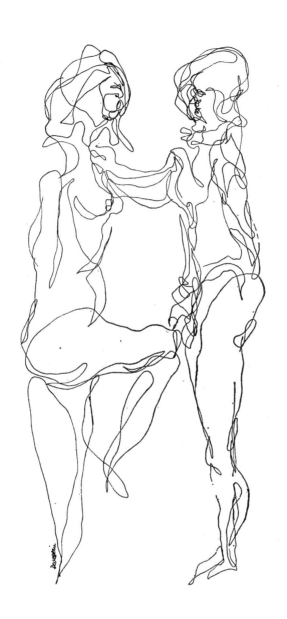

The air of Paradise was the air of dreams, the air that induces man to dream to believe his dreams, the air which casts that spell of "drowsy numbness" whereby all is truth and all is beauty, and beauty and truth are one, within the mind that sleeps and is awake and is awake but sleeps in that land that is the world, and the world that is that land of dreams, and truth and beauty are within and without in all that land that is the world and in that slow and sweetly flowing and all suffusing and sensuous mood which is the only mood in which, one and all, every Adam and every son of Adam and every Eve and every daughter of Eve can know, and feel, and touch, and hear, and smell Paradise, Paradise under their feet, before their eyes, above and beyond them, and everywhere and within them. With hearts that did not ache, and which had not learned the lessons of hearts that ache, with hearts that did not know how to ache, Adam and his Woman breathed and felt that very ambrosial air of Paradise and the Garden of Eden and neither the one nor the other even knew that there was any other kind of air. All they knew was that this was life, and life was Paradise and Paradise was the Garden of Eden, and Adam was the master of the Garden by seal and fiat and the Word of the Lord God, Jehovah, Himself.

But Paradise in the Garden of Eden was not a quiet, silent world. With the beasts of the field and the fowl and birds in the air, fed and increasing and multiplying, the very air was rent by the roars and screeches and howls and neighs and many other noises of lions and tigers, jackasses and cows, cats and dogs, horses, birds, singing canaries and parakeets, humming bees, crazy screeching monkeys, lonely wolves and lambs which had not as yet become poor little lambs, Paradise was full of the cries of life of all of the living world which was created before Adam had been shaped from dust. And even the leaves were stirring and the flowers waved in that ambrosial air, and amidst the noise of life and surrounded by and living amidst the deluging colors of the world, what did the naked Adam say to his naked Woman? What did he tell her? Ay, there's the rub that could have rubbed all of the rub out of the rub of Shakespeare's Hamlet who was only to be conceived eons after the first rub of Adam and his woman.

What did he tell her when she, his unneeded rib made into the flesh of Woman, first saw her lord and master, naked like herself?

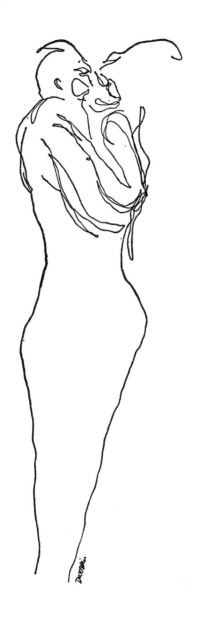

Or did Adam know what to say?

But the serpent did know what to say.

Ye shall not surely die the serpent said unto the Woman.

The serpent talked more, and the serpent said unto the Woman. . . .

"Your eyes shall be opened, and ye shall be as gods, knowing good and evil."

The Woman saw the tree with the red apple, good for food, pleasant to her eyes. She ate. She must have talked to Adam. For he ate.

And thus it all began, because the serpent outtalked Adam, who does not seem to have known what to say.

The serpent has gone unrewarded and forever after, the serpent's successors have been snakes in the grass and have slid along the earth in dirt and slime and mud. And Adam and Eve hid in the shame of their nakedness and the Lord God, Himself, and his angels drove Adam and his Woman out of Paradise, and even made them clothes with which to cover their nakedness. Then Adam worked by the sweat of his brow and the Lord God, Himself, Jehovah, put the desire in Adam, and in sorrow the Woman bore the children which were the fruit, not of Adam's rib, but of his desire. And thus, the Woman

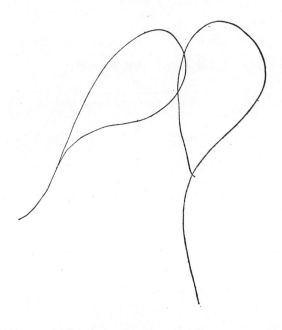

became Eve, Mother Eve, and thus Adam found the Old Adam within himself.

Adam worked hard and lived a long time and was the begetter of more sons, and apparently more daughters, than just about any of the sons of Adam, and Eve begat them all in sorrow and pain. And ever since, the sons of Adam and the sons of the sons of Adam and the daughters of Eve and the daughters of the daughters of Eve have been at it.